WHY WIND

AND WATER FIGHT

AN AFRICAN-AMERICAN TALE

Rewritten by Carole Gerber

Illustrated by Brenden Taylor

Have you seen Wind and Water pitch a fit?

Wind howls at Water.

Water spits at Wind.

One thing leads to another.

Then—uh, oh! They start throwing things

out of pure meanness.

But this wasn't always so.

Oh, no!

In the old days, when Wind felt dry,

Water offered her a drink.

When Water overflowed her banks,

Wind carried her back.

Wind whispered sweetly to Water.

Water bubbled softly to Wind.

Until their grandchildren came along,

they were the best of friends.

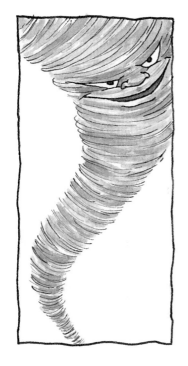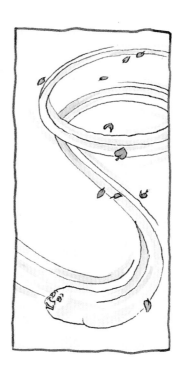

"My grandchildren are such a pleasure!"

Wind was fond of saying.

"I've so many, and none of them alike.

I've got grandchildren who cry and grandchildren who sing.

I've got grandchildren who scream

and grandchildren who whisper.

Some of my grandbabies race 'round and 'round in circles.

And—good gracious, Water—some are so still

I hardly know they're there. My grandchildren—"

"Aieeeeee!" Water shouted, startling Wind.
Water knew Wind could go on bragging forever
because she didn't need to stop for breath.

"Well, Wind," Water said,

"my grandchildren are my greatest pleasure, too!

Oooooo-weee!

One or another of 'em is always running by

to see me.

They just love their old grandma!

And they are all different colors, shapes, and sizes!"

Water added.

"Some of my long, tall grandchildren are red,

and some of my big, fat grandchildren are blue.

Some of my teensy, tiny grandchildren are green,

but some of my other teensy—"

"Yes, yes," Wind snapped. "I know.

Some of your other teensy, tiny grandchildren are red,

and some are blue.

Well, some of my grandchildren are puffy.

But some of them are so wispy and scrawny

that I worry they'll . . ."

Water stopped listening.

She did not like being interrupted by Wind.

She had heard Wind brag, brag, brag

about her grandchildren

until she was sick and tired of it.

Huh! Anybody with eyes

could see that Water's grandchildren

were better than Wind's.

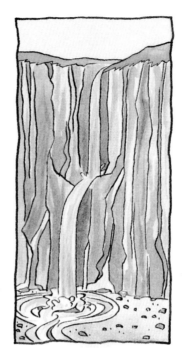

Wind liked to tell

how her grandchildren

came from all different directions.

But Water's grandchildren did, too,

and when they came together,

all her tiny grandchildren

became part of her big, fat, blue grandchildren.

Now that was a trick! Mmm-hmm!

Besides, Water knew
what her grandchildren looked like.
No matter which way she turned,
she could see them running
or falling, or meandering along.
Just thinking of her grandbabies
made Water simmer with contentment.

But Wind's grandchildren?

Huh! They were so rude!

They whipped over her without ever—

not even once—saying,

"Excuse me, Miz Water."

They screamed and danced

when she wanted to rest.

Water couldn't stand them!

Now, Water should have talked with Wind

about her grandchildren's manners.

But she didn't.

Oh, no!

She just got madder and madder and madder.

One day, Wind's grandchildren
skittered rudely over Water
to get a drink.
Water's temper flared.
She grabbed Wind's grandchildren
and wouldn't let go.

When Wind saw what had happened,

she blew on Water and cried,

"Let go of my grandbabies!"

But Water held them tight.

She holds them tight to this very day.

Each time Wind's grandbabies hear her cries,

they twist and turn against Water,

making whitecaps

as they struggle to get free.

Now, when you see a howling wind

batter an angry sea,

you'll understand why Wind and Water fight.